Nana's Silly Goats

by Nancy Lee Mervar
Illustrated by Lori Kiplinger Pandy

To Mom and Dad,
Thank you for a wonderful childhood on our farm.

Publication Information

Text copyright 2010 by Nancy Lee Mervar
Illustration copyright 2010 by Lori Kiplinger Pandy
All rights reserved. No part of this book may be reproduced in any form
or by any electronic or mechanical means, including storage and retrieval
systems, without permission in writing from the author and illustrator.

Library of Congress Cataloging in Publication Data Control Number
2011901048
Mervar, Nancy Lee
Nana's Silly Goats
ISBN 978-0-692-01287-1

Indian Gap Press, PO Box 1069, Lyons, CO 80540-1069
www.indiangappress.com

Consumer Product Safety Improvement Act Information:
Imported by: FedEx Trade Networks (Denver, CO)
            for Indian Gap Press (Lyons, CO)
Sunrise Design & Printing Company, Shenzhen, China; lead free ink
Publication Date: April, 2011, SD11052

Printed in China, First Edition

Acknowledgements

So many people contributed to this simple little
story, and encouraged me along my writing
pathway. This story began as a simple letter to my
mother. I thank my husband, family and friends for
all their support and ideas. Many thanks are also
extended to the teachers and students of Whittier
Elementary International Baccalaureate School in
Boulder, CO, for their comments and suggestions.

Facts about Goats

1) Goats came to America from Europe. The first goats came from Spain.
   Later goats came with the Pilgrims on the Mayflower ship.
2) Rocky Mountain goats are actually goat antelopes.
3) Goats are used for meat and dairy products. Goat milk, butter, yogurt
   and cheese are very tasty and good for you. Goat milk can also be used to make soap.
4) Goats are used to carry packs for hikers.
5) You can knit, crochet, spin and weave goat fiber to make beautiful and
   warm clothes.
6) Goats like to eat grass, leafy branches, bark, and brush. Goats also like to eat weeds like poison ivy. They
   love dandelions! They do not eat tin cans. (Even real goats are not that silly!)
7) Goats do not like to get wet. They need a dry shelter when it rains or snows.
8) Goats are very fun and they are very smart. They are very good at escaping from fences!
9) Pygmy goats are smaller than regular goats and make very good outside pets.
10) Goats are ruminants. They have 4 stomachs. After eating plants for awhile, they ruminate or regurgitate
    the barely digested foods. As they chew their "cud", the plants are properly chewed and swallowed again.

About the Author

Nana (a.k.a. Nancy Lee Mervar) is honored to be the grandma of Erikson, Mandalay and Sedona. She lives on a small ranch in the foothills of the Rocky Mountains with her husband, 13 goats, 6 golden retrievers, and 4 cats.

Dr. Mervar is a retired teacher and principal. She has always loved books, animals and farm life, and teaching. As a young child, Dr. Mervar enjoyed stories read to her by her mother and sisters. She was raised on a small fruit farm in New York State where she spent her childhood outdoors in the woods and fields. All kinds of animals were an important part of that life – chickens, ducks, dogs, cats, pigs, cows, sheep and even one little black goat. Her family participated in 4-H activities and she continues to support this opportunity for youngsters to learn about animals and rural life.

Dr. Mervar's professional life included working with children with special learning needs and their families. She also enjoyed classroom teaching, and administrative roles in both regular and special education. After retiring, Dr. Mervar once again found the time to enjoy animals and rural life, and realized her dream of writing children's books.

To contact the author, visit www.indiangappress.com.

A NEW HOME

 "I miss my kids," said our nana one warm summer day.

Nana had been a teacher and principal. She was used to dozens and dozens of kids. But now she was retired and lived quietly on her mountain with our grandpa.

"We have lots of land to roam, lots of weeds to eat, and a nice warm barn. Let's get some goat kids," reasoned Nana.

Grandpa and Nana bumped along the gravel roads in their big red truck. They were going to a goat ranch.

"Listen," said Nana. "I hear our little ones calling to us."

As Grandpa and Nana got out of their truck, tiny Heidi let out a long, loud bleat. Sammy and Fanny, the other two snow white kids, tilted their heads and butted against Nana's hands. Peter, a brown goat, stood on his back legs and put his hooves on Nana.

"Who are you? What do you want?" asked Fanny and Heidi.

Happy-go-lucky Peter said, "I like you! Can we go home with you?"

But Sammy was not so sure. He wondered, "Will I like a different ranch? Will it be fun there?"

Into the back of the truck
they jumped.

"Blee-eea –t," said Heidi.
"Let's go! Let's go!"

And off they went –
around the curves,
up and down the
hills they traveled
until they reached
Grandpa and Nana's ranch.

First the kids explored their new barn stalls. Fresh wood shavings covered the floor.

Sweet smelling hay filled the manger. Clear cold water shimmered in the bucket.

"Oh, this is nice!" called Peter.

"But look what is through this little door," said Sammy, who was not yet sure about his new home.

He led the other kids out into the sunshine where Grandpa had made a goat playground with tree stumps.

The kids climbed and jumped. Such a fun time!

The playground had tall, fenced walls and even a fenced top.

"Sharing our mountain with us are mountain lions, bobcats, coyotes, owls, hawks and eagles. Your barn and playground will keep you safe," Nana told her kids.

So the kids settled in for a good night's sleep.

The sun woke everyone early the next day.

EXPLORING

"Good morning, little ones," called Nana. "It's time for your first lessons. First you must learn to walk from the barn to the pasture – and remember, no cutting, no butting!"

Peter led the way as he was the oldest and biggest. Fanny and Heidi skipped along behind Peter.

But Sammy said, "I don't want to walk in line. I want to be **FIRST!** "

Outside the barn was a great wide pasture.

Like the little playground, there were fences all around the edges to protect the kids from predators. Instead of stumps and logs, there were huge rocks just right for goat climbing. And best of all, there were so many yummy weeds to eat.

The little goat kids were nervous at first.

"It's okay to explore," said Nana. "Most kids are a little bit afraid when they are someplace new."

After awhile the kids seemed more comfortable. Nana called them to her.

"Do you know the story of Peter Rabbit?" she asked.

The kids scratched their heads with their hind legs and tried to remember the lesson of that story.

"Peter Rabbit was a very curious bunny who liked to explore. Even though he knew it was not safe to visit his neighbor's garden, he went there to play. That was a very silly thing to do. Old Mr. McGregor made Peter into a rabbit pie and ate him all up! You must promise me to stay in your pasture, and not visit the neighbor's fields.

Don't be silly goats!"

Nana left the kids to eat and play. From the deck of her house Nana watched the kids play "King of the Mountain" and other chasing games.

She did not know that Sammy was telling the other kids, "Let's try this yummy grass on the other side of the fence."

Suddenly Nana heard all four kids crying loudly, and she rushed to the pasture.
Peter had remembered the lessons of "Peter Rabbit" very well – perhaps because they shared the same name. Peter stayed safely inside the pasture fence. But Sammy, Fanny and Heidi were now outside the fence, and they were afraid!

"Come back! Come baa-aack," Peter called to his friends.

A few feet in front of the kids stood Old Mr. Cooper.
His hands were on his hips, his feet were wide apart.

"Not a claw, not a paw, not a hoof, not a foot.
NOTHING can come on MY land!" he shouted.

With that he stomped off up the hill.

Sammy, Fanny and Heidi ran to Nana and followed her back inside the fence.

Peter was so happy to see his friends, and they were happy to see him, too.

"Can you tell me what you have learned today?" asked Nana.

"I can lead the other kids from the barn to the pasture," said Peter very proudly.

"And what have you learned, Sammy?" asked Nana.

"It is safer and much nicer to stay in your own pasture!" answered Sammy.

Nana's new kids had learned enough for one day.

All the goats followed Nana from the pasture to the barn – even Sammy. Nana gave them a special corn treat as well as pats and hugs.

As Nana tucked them in for the night, she called, "Good Night, my silly little goats!"

The next day,
the goat kids went outside
to play. Yesterday had been a
scary day, so all the kids promised to
stay inside their pasture and not be silly goats.

Soon they were busy eating, playing and exploring. Little Heidi wiggled down between the big rocks for some particularly tasty weeds.

Overhead a huge shadow blocked out the sun. High above Heidi floated a golden eagle – a very hungry eagle that had spotted movement between the rocks.

Heidi tucked her little head between her hooves and stayed very, very still.

In her imagination she saw all the predators that Nana had described – bobcats, coyotes, hawks, and mountain lions. It was too scary!

The eagle flew lower and lower. He could no longer see what was moving between the rocks.

"What happened to my dinner?" shouted the eagle angrily. He made one more pass over the rocks, and then flew higher into the sky.

As the shadow faded away, Heidi cautiously left the rocks to play with her friends and tell them of her adventure.

She may have made the story just a little bit more scary than it really was, and added just a few more predators than there really were, but isn't that what makes a better story?

Nana had been watching and thought her silly goats had all the adventures they needed. But Grandpa's orange tractor seemed to invite more mischief.

On the front of the tractor was a big loading bucket that Grandpa used for moving rocks, dirt and logs. The little goats thought it was very fun to play there, and sometimes all four kids played in the bucket.

It was also fun to climb up on the seat of the tractor and pretend to drive! Fanny pressed the lever that raised the bucket. Up … up … up in the air went Sammy and Peter. **Bleaaaaaaat!**

Nana was inside the barn filling the kids' dinner dishes with corn. Hearing their cries, she ran out of the barn. Quickly Nana moved Fanny off the tractor and away from the lever.

Ever so slowly, Nana brought the bucket back down to the ground. Out jumped Sammy and Peter! They were so very glad to be back on the ground again.

"Silly goats," said Nana. "Goats are not meant to drive tractors – or to ride into the air!"

Even though her kids got into all kinds of trouble, Nana loved her silly little goats. She liked to sit in the pasture with them and watch them play. She also loved to read stories to them.

One day Nana thought it would be fun to have her friends come for a picnic lunch in the pasture.

"What fun!" said Connie.

"What a good idea," said Debbie.

Together they hiked to the pasture with their sack lunches and chose a nice flat rock to sit on together.

Debbie brought raisins and carrots. Connie brought cookies. And everyone had great big gooey peanut butter and jelly sandwiches.

Nana had never eaten in the pasture with her kids. She was in for a big surprise!

Soon Nana and her friends had silly goats climbing all over them!

Heidi liked the crunchy carrots. Peter loved the sweet raisins. Fanny was sure that the chocolate chip cookies were made just for her. And Sammy –

-- well, Sammy decided to sample a peanut butter
and jelly sandwich. It was very, very sticky inside
his little mouth!

"Blaaaah," said Sammy as he tried to get the
peanut butter out of his mouth.

Nana and her friends
laughed and laughed.

"Silly goats," said Nana.
"Goats are not meant
to eat peanut butter!"

Peter, Sammy, Fanny and Heidi, Nana's silly goats, continued to eat and play each day in their pasture. Some days there was an adventure; some days were just peaceful and calm.

Every night they went to sleep in their safe, warm barn.

And every afternoon, Nana gathered them together to tell the kids stories – for all teachers love to teach, and all kinds of kids love to learn.